Hercu
Pull T

There are more books about the Bailey School Kids!
Have you read these adventures?

#1 Vampires Don't Wear Polka Dots
#2 Werewolves Don't Go to Summer Camp
#3 Santa Claus Doesn't Mop Floors
#4 Leprechauns Don't Play Basketball
#5 Ghosts Don't Eat Potato Chips
#6 Frankenstein Doesn't Plant Petunias
#7 Aliens Don't Wear Braces
#8 Genies Don't Ride Bicycles
#9 Pirates Don't Wear Pink Sunglasses
#10 Witches Don't Do Backflips
#11 Skeletons Don't Play Tubas
#12 Cupid Doesn't Flip Hamburgers
#13 Gremlins Don't Chew Bubble Gum
#14 Monsters Don't Scuba Dive
#15 Zombies Don't Play Soccer
#16 Dracula Doesn't Drink Lemonade
#17 Elves Don't Wear Hard Hats
#18 Martians Don't Take Temperatures
#19 Gargoyles Don't Ride School Buses
#20 Wizards Don't Need Computers
#21 Mummies Don't Coach Softball
#22 Cyclops Doesn't Roller-Skate
#23 Angels Don't Know Karate
#24 Dragons Don't Cook Pizza
#25 Bigfoot Doesn't Square Dance
#26 Mermaids Don't Run Track
#27 Bogeymen Don't Play Football
#28 Unicorns Don't Give Sleigh Rides
#29 Knights Don't Teach Piano

The Bailey School Kids Joke Book
Super Special #1: Mrs. Jeepers Is Missing!
Super Special #2: Mrs. Jeepers' Batty Vacation

Hercules Doesn't Pull Teeth

by Debbie Dadey
and
Marcia Thornton Jones

illustrated by John Steven Gurney

SCHOLASTIC INC.
New York Toronto London Auckland Sydney

ISBN 0-590-25809-5

12 11 10 9 0 1/0 2/0 3/0

Printed in the U.S.A. 40

First Scholastic printing, March 1998

Book design by Laurie Williams

To Robert Jared Thornton —
my weight-lifting nephew! — MTJ

For my strong older brother, Frank Gibson — DD

Contents

1

Dr. Zeus

"What kind of dumb name is that?" Eddie asked. "It sounds like a disease."

"It's my dentist's name," Liza explained as she pointed to the building directory. "Dr. Zeus has always been my dentist. He's very old and very nice." Eddie, Liza, and their friends Melody and Howie got on the elevator to go up to the twelfth floor. Liza had an after-school appointment with the dentist and her friends were coming with her.

"There's no such thing as a nice dentist," Eddie muttered, pulling off his baseball cap. "All they want to do is poke your gums until they bleed."

"That's not true," Liza said. "Dr. Zeus is very gentle."

Howie pushed button number twelve

on the elevator. "Zeus is a very famous name," he told Eddie.

"I know," Melody said. "It's from ancient Greece. There are stories about Zeus as a mighty god."

Eddie looked at Melody like she had sprouted carrots out her ears. "How did you know that?" Eddie asked.

Melody put her hands on her hips and tossed her black braids behind her shoulders. "I know lots of stuff. Zeus was the most important of the Greek gods. He's on a trading card I have at home. I have one for Zeus, another one for this creature called Medusa that has snakes on her head, and another one —"

"I think you have rocks in your head," Eddie joked. "Who cares about some dead guy that lived zillions of years ago?"

Melody shrugged. "Some of the stories on the back of the cards are neat."

The door to the elevator opened and the four kids walked into room 1212.

Thick purple carpets covered the floor and big gold chairs lined the walls. Heavy purple curtains were pulled back from the window with giant gold chains.

"Wow," Eddie said. "This guy must be super rich. His office looks like a palace. Maybe I should be a dentist when I grow up."

Howie smiled. "I could be a doctor right next door to you." Howie had wanted to be a doctor since he'd been in kindergarten.

Eddie stabbed a finger toward Liza's mouth. "I could jab you in the jaw and you'd pay me money for it."

Liza shook her head. "Every other dentist would have to be dead before I'd let you put one grubby paw in my mouth."

"You'd better tell the receptionist you're here," Melody told Liza. Liza nodded and walked up to a window inside the waiting room. When Liza returned she was pale.

"What's wrong?" Melody asked.

1212

"You look like someone ate your tongue," Eddie joked.

Liza looked like she was about to cry. "The most horrible thing in the world has happened!"

2

Lucky Twelve

"The television station broke down?" Eddie asked.

"I'm serious," Liza said.

"So am I," Eddie told her. "No television is the most horrible thing I can think of."

Howie patted Liza on the shoulder "What's wrong? Did the dentist cancel your appointment?"

Liza shook her head. "Worse," she said. "Dr. Zeus is missing."

"MISSING!" Melody shrieked. "Have the police been called?"

"Maybe they should hire a private detective," Eddie suggested. "They could use bloodhounds to sniff out his trail."

"They only use bloodhounds to sniff

out escaped criminals," Howie pointed out.

"People who pull teeth and drill holes in them sound like criminals to me," Eddie said matter-of-factly.

Howie was ready to argue with Eddie, but Liza interrupted. "Dr. Zeus is not a criminal. He's the best dentist in the world. Or at least he was until last week," Liza said sadly. "He retired and flew someplace sunny."

Eddie put his hands on his hips. "You told us he was missing!" Eddie said. "All he did was quit! What's wrong with that?"

"Now I have to see the new dentist," Liza said. She still looked ready to cry.

Melody shrugged. "I'm sure Dr. Zeus was careful about picking his replacement."

Liza sniffed and nodded. "The nurse told me the new dentist is his son. The receptionist said he would see me in twelve minutes."

"Twelve?" Howie asked. "That's weird."

"It looks like the new tooth dude in town likes the number twelve," Eddie said, pointing to the waiting room.

Melody, Liza, and Howie counted. "Twelve gold chairs," Howie said.

"There are twelve pictures on the wall, too," Melody said.

"That's strange," Howie said.

Eddie rolled his eyes. "If you ask me, twelve is better than unlucky thirteen!"

"Eddie's right," Melody said. "There is nothing to worry about."

Just then, a door squeaked open. "I am ready to see you now," a deep voice rumbled.

When the four kids turned around, they found themselves facing a giant.

3

Dr. Herb

The man was so tall he had to duck to get through the door. It only took him three steps to reach the kids. He towered over them and held out his hand.

"I am Dr. Herb," he said. "Your new dentist."

Liza's hand looked tiny when she shook Dr. Herb's hand. "I'm pleased to meet you," she said, but her voice shook.

Dr. Herb smiled. "No need to be scared," he said. "My father taught me everything he knew."

A super-sized white dentist's jacket covered Dr. Herb's watermelon-sized muscles. Right over his bulging chest muscles on the left side was a badge showing a picture of Earth. Purple letters

CHAMPION
OF THE WORLD

on the badge said: CHAMPION OF THE WORLD.

"I thought Atlas was the champion," Melody said. She remembered the legend of a strong man named Atlas who held up the world.

"Don't you know anything?" Eddie said. "An atlas is a book with maps in it."

Dr. Herb laughed so loud the glass in the door rattled. "Atlas needs no maps. He won't be going anywhere for a long, long time. But you," he said, pointing to Liza, "need to be going to room twelve so I can shine your teeth!"

Liza took a deep breath. "I'll be out soon," she told her friends.

Eddie nodded. "This guy will be quick. After all, he's so strong, he could pull a tooth with one flick of his pinkie."

Liza's hands flew to her mouth. "I don't need any teeth pulled," she mumbled through her fingers.

"You look as scared as my puppy did last summer," Dr. Herb said with a laugh.

"Boy, was he hot under his collar when I caught him. But I brought him home and now he's as lazy as a grizzly bear in winter."

Howie stood up tall. "I saved a homeless puppy, too," he said.

"Well," Dr. Herb said with a laugh. "My dog, Cerb, is happy to live with me, just as I'm sure Liza will be happy to have her teeth sparkling white." Dr. Herb held up ten fingers. Then he flashed two fingers. "She'll be out in twelve minutes," he said.

And then Dr. Herb and Liza disappeared through the door.

4

Cerb

"Do you think she'll be okay?" Melody asked. "Dr. Herb is the biggest dentist I've ever seen."

"He's the professional wrestler of the teeth-pulling world," Eddie agreed.

"I'm sure she'll be fine," Howie assured Melody.

"She's not having brain surgery," Eddie said. "She's only getting her teeth cleaned. Why don't we go play soccer while she's in there?"

Howie shook his head. "Dr. Herb said she'd only be twelve minutes. We wouldn't even have time to get downstairs from the twelfth floor before she was done."

"Dr. Herb sure likes the number twelve," Melody said. "If you ask me, it's a little strange."

Eddie stared at a picture on the wall. "This dog is a little strange, if you ask me." Howie and Melody looked at the picture, too. A huge brown dog with yellow eyes stared back at them. A gold plate under the picture had four letters: CERB.

"That's a weird name for a dog," Howie said.

Melody looked around the room and gulped. She pointed to two more pictures of huge dogs. Both dogs were brown and

ferocious looking. Underneath each picture were the letters: CERB.

"It looks like an ugly dog convention to me," Eddie joked.

"Don't you think it's pretty strange that Dr. Herb has three dogs named Cerb?" Melody asked.

"Maybe he likes rhyming names," Howie suggested. "Cerb rhymes with Herb."

"Maybe he's lazy," Eddie said. "He could call all three dogs just by yelling Cerb once."

Melody looked around the room at the heavy purple drapes and the thick gold chains pulling them back. "Isn't purple a royal color?" she asked.

Howie nodded. "Kings and queens in the olden days wore purple for big ceremonies. No one else was allowed to wear purple."

"This place is giving me the creeps," Melody said. "I'm getting worried about Liza. I better check on her."

Howie looked at his watch. "I don't think it's been twelve minutes yet."

Melody didn't stop to think about the time. She just barged into room twelve and came face-to-face with a three-headed dog.

5

Greek Gods

"You didn't have to scream your head off," Liza told Melody after leaving the dentist's office. The kids were in the elevator going down from the twelfth floor. "It was only a statue of a dog."

Melody pushed her black braids out of her face and shrugged. "It surprised me, that's all."

"Why did you come into the examining room in the first place?" Liza asked. "I was almost done. Dr. Herb must have a magic toothbrush. I've never had my teeth cleaned so fast."

Eddie bopped Melody on the head with his baseball cap. "Melody was worried that King Kong dentist would carry you off to the Empire State Building," he told Liza.

"You have to admit, Dr. Herb is different from most dentists," Melody said.

"Nothing is wrong with being different," Liza pointed out.

The four kids stepped off the elevator and Melody pulled them close. "There is nothing wrong with being different, but there is something wrong with keeping a three-headed dog prisoner," she told her friends.

"What are you talking about?" Howie asked.

Eddie shook his head. "She's flipped out. She's lost her marbles. She's living in la-la land."

Melody put her hands on her hips. "I'm perfectly fine. Come to my house and I'll show you what I'm talking about."

"I want to play soccer," Eddie complained.

"I do, too," Melody told him. "But this is important."

"So is soccer," Eddie told her, but he trudged alongside his friends to Melody's house. In her room, Melody pulled out a big box of trading cards from under her bed.

Eddie's eyes lit up. "Now you're talking. I'll go home and get my baseball cards and we can trade."

"No," Melody said. "These aren't to trade. Just look." Melody spread purple and gold cards out on her floor. Across the top of each card were gold letters that said: GREEK GODS AND GODDESSES. Every card had a different picture. There

GREEK GODS AND GODDESSES
ZEUS
GREEK GODS AND GODDESSES
HERCULES

was one of a strong man holding a lightning bolt. Purple letters at the bottom named him ZEUS.

Liza pointed at the name Zeus. "Hey, that's my old dentist's name."

Melody pointed to another card. It had a young man with bulging muscles carrying a lion on his shoulder.

"Big deal," Eddie said. "He has muscles, but what's his batting average?"

"They didn't have baseball back in those days," Howie explained. "That's Hercules. He was the strongest man in the world."

Melody nodded. "He had to perform twelve superhuman labors in twelve years. He did things no ordinary human could do."

"If he was so great, he should have played sports," Eddie said. "Then he could have been really famous."

Liza picked up the card. "Hercules *is* famous. But I don't understand why you wanted to show us these cards."

"Because," Melody said slowly, "I think Dr. Herb is . . ."

"Is who?" Eddie asked impatiently.

Melody grabbed the card from Liza. "Dr. Herb is Hercules!"

6

Underworld Pets

Howie and Liza giggled, but Eddie laughed right out loud. He laughed so hard he rolled on the floor, grabbing a handful of Melody's trading cards and throwing them high in the air. One of the cards floated down and bopped Howie on top of his head.

Howie stopped laughing when he saw the picture on the card.

"Hey," Howie shouted.

Eddie, Liza, and Melody all froze and stared at their friend. "What's wrong?" Liza asked. "You look like you just found out you need four teeth pulled!"

"That wouldn't bother me," Howie said, "as long as I knew the dentist didn't get his pets in the underworld."

"Most pets don't live underwater," Eddie said.

"I'm not talking about water," Howie said. "I'm talking about the evil underworld."

"You must mean under Eddie's bed," Liza said with a giggle.

"No," Melody said. "Hercules captured the three-headed dog that guarded the underworld. It was the last of his twelve challenges."

"Big deal," Eddie said. "Hercules probably left a trail of doggy treats. Even I could figure that out and I'm not Hercules."

"I hope you're right," Howie said. "But then, how do you explain this?"

Howie tossed the card on the floor in front of his friends. It landed faceup, showing a picture of a mean-looking dog with three heads. "Look close," Howie told his friends. Liza, Melody, and Eddie bent low over the picture.

"Its name is Cerberus," Howie pointed out.

"My name is Eddie," Eddie said. "And your name must be Larry Lunatic."

Liza nodded. "You sound as crazy as Melody."

"I'm not crazy!" Melody said. "Dr. Herb is very strange."

"She's right," Howie said. "Liza's dentist has three pictures of dogs named Cerb that look just like the monster dog on this trading card. I think Cerb is short for Cerberus!"

Melody clapped her hands. "I bet after Hercules got back from the underworld everybody was afraid of the three-headed dog so he decided to keep it as a pet. The pictures in his office are of Cerberus!"

"Dr. Herb is not keeping a three-headed monster as a pet," Eddie said. "He just has three different dogs with the same name."

"Exactly," Liza said. "Just like there have been lots of dogs named Lassie."

Howie shook his head. "There's something fishy about Dr. Herb," he said. "We have to get to the bottom of it!"

7

The Weight of the Sky

"It's all your fault," Melody snapped.

Liza shrugged. "I didn't do anything," she said.

"Yes, you did," Melody argued. "You told my mom about Dr. Herb and that reminded her that I haven't been to a dentist in a long time. Now I have to go to Dr. Herb, and I bet he finds a cavity." Melody held her hand to her cheek and moaned.

Melody and her three friends met in their favorite place, under the giant oak tree on the Bailey School playground. They were supposed to play soccer, but Melody had to go to the dentist instead.

"Do you have a toothache?" Howie asked.

"No," Melody said. "But I bet I will after Dr. Herb is finished with me."

"The worst part," Eddie said, "is that you'll be sitting in a stuffy dentist's office instead of playing soccer."

"No fair," Melody cried. "You went to the dentist with Liza. Now you should go with me. We can play when I get finished with the dentist."

"Oh, no," Eddie said, backing away from Melody. "I'm not hanging around a tooth driller's torture chamber again when I could be playing soccer!"

"Wait," Howie said. "Melody has a point."

"So does the dentist," Eddie said. "And it drills right down into raw nerves."

Melody screamed and covered her mouth with her hands.

"Stop it," Liza said. "Dr. Herb won't hurt Melody. And it won't hurt us to go with her."

"Aw, shucks," Eddie said, kicking at the

trunk of the oak tree. "There goes my soccer game."

"It'll be worth it," Liza said, "when you see Melody's sparkling smile."

Eddie grumbled all the way to the dentist, but his three friends ignored him. They rode the elevator to the twelfth floor and settled into the chairs in office 1212. In twelve minutes, Dr. Herb beamed at them and Melody disappeared down the hallway to get her teeth cleaned.

Melody scooted past the statue of Cerberus and settled into the dentist's chair. "You look very tired," Melody said when Dr. Herb stretched his back.

"It has been a busy week," Dr. Herb said. "You're my tenth patient and my back is killing me. I feel like I've been holding up the weight of the sky."

"That would make you Atlas," Melody said.

Dr. Herb frowned. "That Atlas, he al-

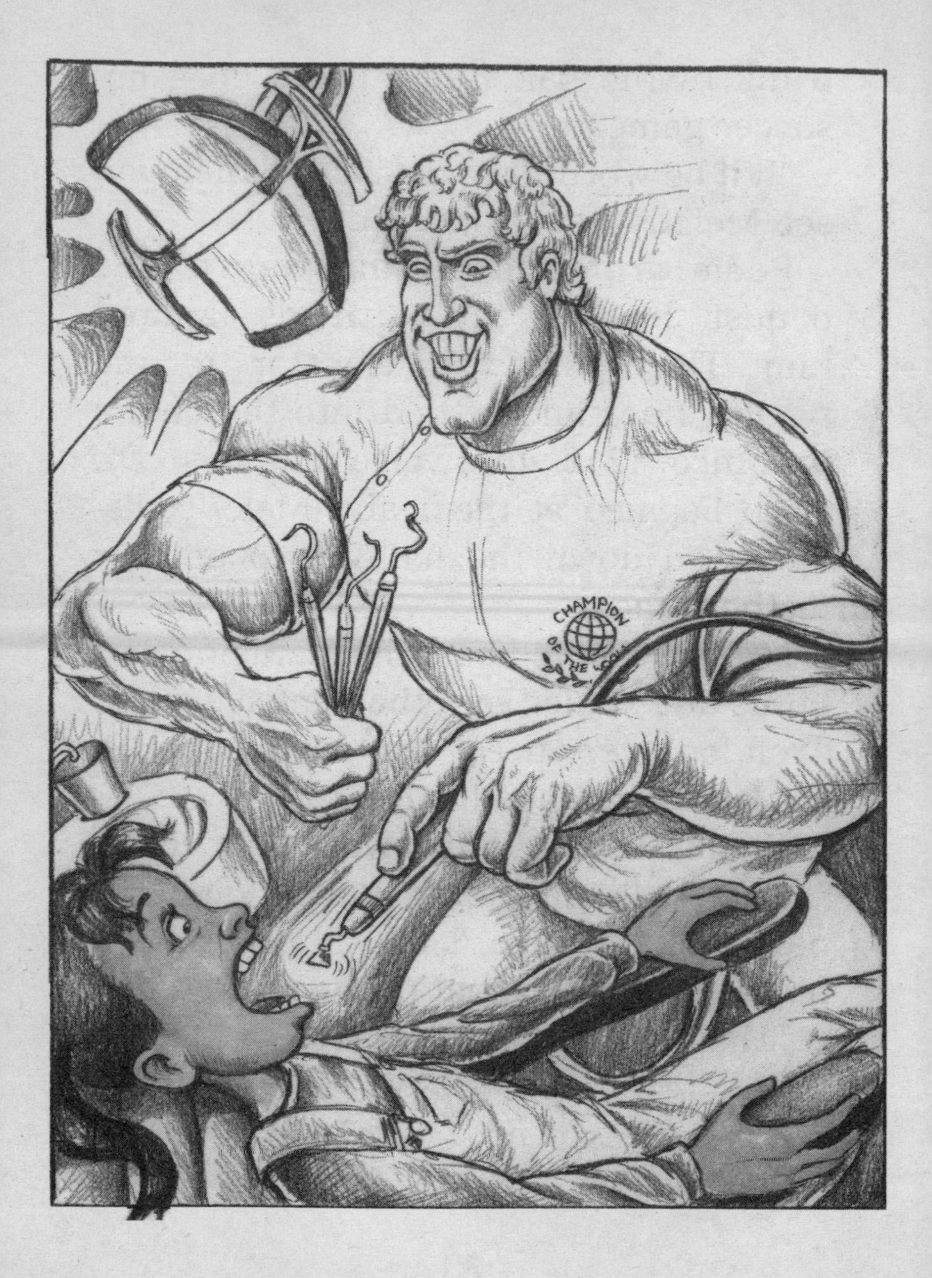
CHAMPION
OF THE

ways gets the credit," Dr. Herb growled. "He never admits he had help!"

Melody gulped. "I didn't mean to make you mad," she said.

Dr. Herb shrugged. "I'm not angry at you," he said. "But I've been on many journeys and it's the same wherever I go. The wrong person gets all the credit."

"That's not always true," Melody said. "When people work hard they get credit in Bailey City."

"Exactly!" Dr. Herb said and pounded his fist on the counter. When he did, the toothbrush he was holding snapped in two. "That's why I came here. I plan to clean out Bailey City!"

Melody whimpered. "Clean out?"

Dr. Herb looked at Melody and smiled. "I'm talking about teeth!" he said. "My challenge is to check every tooth in Bailey City. And you're next on the list!"

And then Dr. Herb came straight at Melody.

8

Superhuman Muscle Men

When Melody ran down the hallway and burst into the waiting room, her friends jumped up. "What's wrong?" Liza asked. "Do you have a cavity?"

Melody glanced over her shoulder and moaned. She grabbed Howie's and Liza's arms and pulled them out the door of office 1212. Eddie followed close behind.

"Do you have to get braces?" Eddie asked.

Melody shook her head, but she didn't answer until they were safely on the elevator. "I wish it was just a cavity or braces," Melody said.

"Going to the dentist isn't as fun as playing soccer," Liza admitted. "But it's nothing to be so scared about."

"It *is* scary when the dentist is Hercules," Melody said as they left the office building. "And he's planning on taking over Bailey City."

"Not that strongman story again," Eddie complained. "I'm pretty sure Dr. Herb is not Hercules," he said. "After all, Hercules doesn't pull teeth."

Liza giggled. "Eddie's right. Hercules is a made-up story. There are no such things as superhuman muscle men and dogs with three heads."

"But he told me he was here on a challenge," Melody argued. "A challenge is just like the labors Hercules had to complete."

"Did he really say he was going to take over Bailey City?" Howie asked.

Melody pulled her friends into the shadow of a nearby building. "I figured out he plans to crush the other dentists in town," Melody whispered. "It's up to us to stop him!"

"This is worse than I thought," Eddie said.

BAILEY CITY PLA

“Then you believe Melody?” Liza asked.

“No,” Eddie said. “This is worse because Melody is beyond crazy. Her brain has turned into toothpaste!”

“If you’re so sure Dr. Herb is a normal dentist,” Howie said slowly, “then you won’t be scared to prove it.”

“The only thing I’m scared of is Melody’s brains oozing out her ears,” Eddie said.

“Okay,” Howie said. “Then I have a plan. We’ll follow Dr. Herb home.”

“What will that prove?” Liza asked.

Melody grabbed Liza’s arm. “I know,” Melody whispered. “If we find out where Dr. Herb lives, we’ll see his three-headed dog.”

“There is no three-headed monster dog,” Liza said, “except in your imagination.”

“Then you’ll go?” Howie asked.

“I’ll do anything,” Eddie said, “to get you to stop talking this Hercules nonsense.”

Howie and Melody nodded. "We'll meet here," Melody said, "just as the sun is setting."

"Fine," Eddie said. "I'll be ready."

"Ready to fight Hercules?" Liza asked.

"No," Eddie said. "Ready to prove Melody and Howie are wrong!"

9

Home for Hercules

"There he is," Melody whispered as Dr. Herb came out of the office building.

"We can't follow him," Liza said as the last bit of sunlight faded in the sky. "Eddie isn't here yet."

"Maybe he decided not to come," Howie said. "After all, he didn't believe us."

"But Eddie loves to spy," Liza said. "We should wait for him."

"If we don't follow Dr. Herb now," Melody said, "we'll never know where he lives."

Melody, Liza, and Howie stayed in the shadows as they walked down Green Street past the Bailey City Mall. Dr. Herb whistled as he walked and never once looked behind him. On his shoulder, Dr.

Herb carried a huge suitcase that was big enough to hold a ten-year-old kid.

"I don't like this," Liza whispered. They were right across from the Bailey City Cemetery when a dog barked. Another dog barked, then another. Finally, three dogs barked together.

"Maybe that's Cerb, Cerb, and Cerb," Liza whimpered.

Howie put his hand on Liza's shoulder. "I thought you didn't believe in three-headed dogs," he said.

"When it starts to get dark and I'm right beside a cemetery, anything is possible," Liza said with a gulp. "I want to go home."

"We can't leave now," Melody said. "I think Dr. Herb is almost home." She pointed ahead to Dr. Herb. He turned onto Olympus Lane.

"Wow," Howie said. "He really is rich." Olympus Lane only had a few houses on it, and every house was like a palace. Dr. Herb went up the driveway of a huge

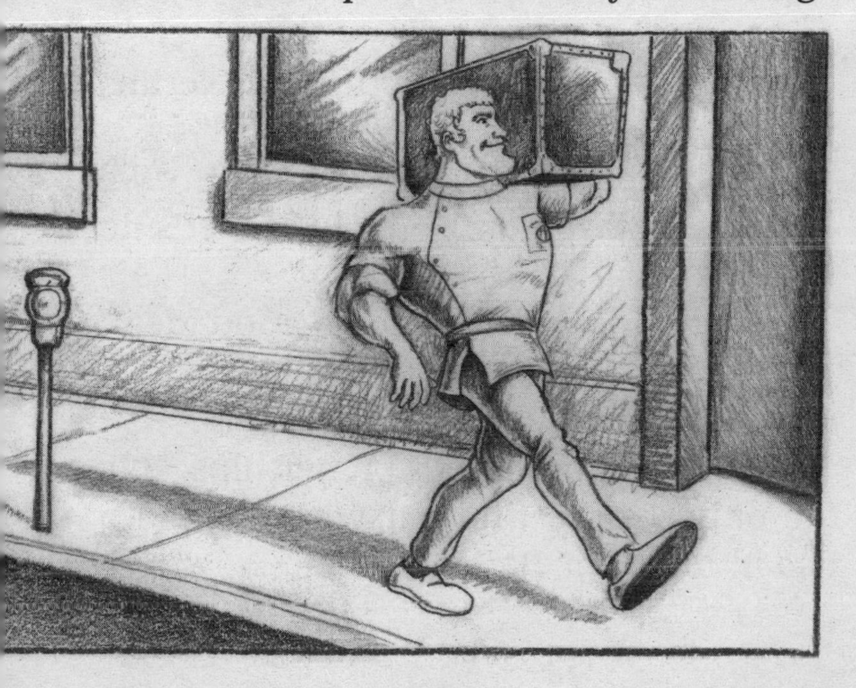

three-story home that had at least ten columns holding up the porch roof.

"Of course he's rich," Melody said. "He is the son of a king."

"King?" Liza asked. "I thought he was the son of a dentist."

Melody rolled her eyes. "Didn't you read my trading cards? Zeus was the king of all the Greek gods and Hercules was Zeus' son."

"Cool," Howie said. "That means royalty cleaned your teeth. Does a queen cut your hair?"

Liza giggled. "Maybe a princess scrubs your toilets."

"Very funny," Melody snapped. "We came here to spy on Hercules, so let's do it."

"I don't think this is such a good idea," Liza said. "Spying is not very nice. It might even be against the law."

Melody put her hands on her hips. "It's the only way to find out what Dr. Herb has in mind for Bailey City."

"And *if* he's really Hercules," Howie added. "Besides, we're not going to hurt anybody."

Liza nodded. "I suppose you're right."

"Be quiet," Melody told her friends. "We have to keep our eyes and ears open for anything unusual."

The three kids were silent for a minute, watching the lights come on in the big house, when suddenly Liza pulled on Melody's sleeve. "Would something moving in the bushes be unusual?" Liza squeaked.

"Sure," Melody said. "Where are the bushes moving?"

Liza looked ready to faint. "Right behind us." Liza gulped. "And whatever it is, it's getting closer!"

10

One Bite

"Oh, my gosh," Liza squealed. "It's Cerberus and it's going to eat us alive!"

Howie's face was pale. "Cerberus could swallow all three of us in one bite."

Melody grabbed a stick from the ground. "It's not going to make me doggie kibble without a fight." Liza and Howie grabbed sticks, too, and held them up like King Arthur's knights with swords.

"Great," Howie said with a trembling voice. "All we have to fight off a dragon-eating monster with are these little toothpicks."

"Let's hope it is a dragon-eating monster and not a kid-eating monster," Liza said as the bushes right beside them shook.

All three kids jumped as a figure leaped out of the bushes at them.

"AHHH!" they screamed.

"Shhh," Eddie said. "Do you want everyone on Olympus Lane to know we're here?"

"Eddie," Liza scolded. "You almost gave me a heart attack. I thought you were a killer dog."

"My grandmother thinks I'm a mad dog," Eddie said with a grin. "But that's only when I'm foaming at the mouth with toothpaste."

Melody punched Eddie in the arm. "What's the big idea of sneaking up on us like that?" she asked.

"I got to Dr. Herb's building just as you were leaving, so I followed you," Eddie explained. "Have you seen anything yet?"

Howie shook his head. "It just looks like an ordinary rich person's house to me."

"Maybe these will help," Eddie said, holding up a big pair of black binoculars. "They're my dad's." Eddie lifted the binoculars to his eyes and concentrated on Dr. Herb's house.

"Wow," Eddie said. "That box Dr. Herb carried home is big enough for . . ."

"Big enough for what?" Liza asked.

"Big enough to put one of his patients in," Eddie said seriously.

"I don't think Hercules ever really hurt anyone, did he?" Melody asked.

"You can't be the strongest man in the world and fight battles without knocking a few heads together," Howie said.

"Shhh," Eddie said. "Dr. Herb is doing something."

"Is he beating up somebody?" Liza asked.

"No," Eddie said. "He's dusting."

"Dusting!" Melody, Liza, and Howie exclaimed together.

"What kind of muscle man dusts?" Melody said.

Eddie continued staring through the binoculars. "A very boring one," Eddie said. "I told you he's just a dumb old dentist."

"What's he dusting?" Melody asked.

"Old stuff," Eddie said. "It looks like an old sword, a globe, and this big gold crown on a stand."

"A prince would have a crown," Howie said.

"It's just a piece of junk," Eddie said. "It must be a zillion years old. Wait! Now he's doing something exciting."

"Is he putting on the crown?" Liza asked.

Eddie frowned and put down his binoculars. "He may be a dentist, but he's not a sissy. He's lifting weights."

"What's wrong with that?" Liza said.

Eddie pulled off his baseball cap and scratched his head. "Maybe Dr. Herb really is Hercules," he said. "I just saw him lift more weights than ten men could lift. And he did it with one hand."

"Let me see those binoculars," Melody said, grabbing them away from Eddie. Melody peered through the binoculars at Dr. Herb.

"What's he doing now?" Liza asked.

Melody gulped before answering. "He's coming out the door and heading straight toward us!"

11

Magic Number

"Let's get out of here," Howie said.

"Run!" Eddie yelled. Eddie cut through the bushes and raced into the dark shadows of the cemetery.

"Where are you going?" Melody screamed.

"This is a shortcut," Eddie hollered over his shoulder. "Follow me."

Melody, Howie, and Liza zigzagged through the cemetery after their friend. Melody and Howie kept up with Eddie, but Liza fell behind. Soon, her friends were out of sight.

"Stop!" Liza panted. "Wait for me!" Liza leaned against a tree. She crouched low and held her breath when she heard footsteps pounding the dirt.

"Liza?" Melody hissed through the darkness. "Where did you go?"

Liza let out her breath with a big whoosh. "I'm over here," she whispered.

Melody, Howie, and Eddie appeared in front of Liza. "Why did you stop?" Eddie snapped.

Melody pulled on Eddie's shirt until he plopped down on the ground next to her. "We need to rest," Melody said. "Or Hercules will catch us for sure."

"The only person that's going to catch us is a mad dentist," Eddie told her.

"Why did you run if you didn't believe he's Hercules?" Liza asked.

"Because the last person I want mad at me is a dentist," Eddie said.

"Maybe he didn't see us," Liza said hopefully. But no one answered her because just then they heard something that sent goose bumps racing up their backs. Three different dogs were barking, and they were heading their way.

"Hercules is siccing Cerberus on us,"

Melody said. "We have to get out of here."

"If that really is Cerberus and Hercules, we might as well give up," Liza said. "We can't outrun monsters like that!"

"No," Eddie said. "But we can outwit them!"

Melody, Liza, and Howie stared at their friend. "*You* plan to outwit them?" Melody asked.

Eddie sat up straight. "I'm not stupid," he said. "I happen to have lots of good ideas."

"Yes," Liza admitted. "But most of your ideas are mean or downright dangerous."

"Not this one," Eddie said. "All we have to do is split up in four directions and make our way to the oak tree on the playground."

"What good will that do?" Liza said.

"I get it," Howie said. "Cerberus may have three heads, but he only has one body. Splitting up will confuse him."

Melody nodded. "I hope it works."

"We're about to find out," Howie said, "because Cerberus is almost here. Let's go!"

The four friends raced away in different directions. They hadn't gone far when they heard the barks change into yelps and whimpers. When the kids met up under the oak tree they were out of breath, but they were all right.

"Eddie," Liza said, "I owe you an apology. Your plan was brilliant!"

Eddie smiled and gave a little bow.

"Don't start bragging," Melody said, "unless you have another plan for getting rid of Hercules for good."

"Eddie doesn't have to think of a plan," Howie said slowly, "because I just thought of something. Twelve seems to be a magic number for Dr. Herb and Hercules," Howie explained. "We know Melody was

Dr. Herb's tenth patient. What happens when he gets to patient number twelve?"

Eddie shrugged. "I guess we'll never know," he said.

"Yes, we will," Howie said with a grin. "Because I plan on being patient eleven."

"Well, if you're patient eleven, who will be twelve?" Eddie asked.

Melody, Liza, and Howie didn't say a word. Instead, they stared at Eddie.

Eddie's hands covered his mouth. "You can't be serious," he said through his fingers.

"We're serious," Melody said slowly. "Deadly serious!"

12

Patient Number Twelve

"I can't believe you're making me do this," Eddie grumbled. "My grandmother took my temperature when I told her I was making an appointment with a dentist. She thought I was sick with a fever."

Eddie and his friends Melody, Howie, and Liza were riding the elevator up to the twelfth floor. Howie had already made an appointment for right after school. Eddie was going to make his appointment when they got there. The elevator doors slid open and the four friends quietly walked into office 1212. Howie, Liza, and Melody stood with Eddie while he made an appointment. Then Howie told the receptionist he was ready.

"What if he starts drilling holes in my teeth?" Eddie asked.

Liza giggled. "A few more holes in your head shouldn't hurt anything!"

"This is nothing to laugh about," Eddie told her. "I could be hurt in there!"

Liza's eyes got big, then she started giggling.

"Now what's so funny?" Melody asked.

"Who would ever have thought," Liza gasped, "that Eddie's afraid of the dentist!"

"I am not," Eddie snapped.

"Then stop worrying," Liza told him. "Dr. Herb is as gentle as a kitten when he's cleaning teeth."

Howie snapped his fingers. "I just thought of another plan, and if it works Eddie won't have to worry about seeing the dentist. At least, not today."

"What are you going to do?" Melody asked.

Howie didn't answer her because the door leading to the examining rooms swung open and Dr. Herb grinned down at the four friends. “I am ready for you now,” Dr. Herb said. “Please, follow me.”

Howie slowly followed Dr. Herb. He squeezed past the three-headed dog statue and slid into the dentist’s chair. Before Dr. Herb could begin cleaning his teeth, Howie started talking. “You really have big muscles,” he told Dr. Herb.

“I work out with weights,” Dr. Herb said. Then he pinched Howie’s skinny arm. “I could teach you how to work your muscles if you’d like.”

Howie sighed. “I could never be as strong as you. I bet you could lift an entire car.”

Dr. Herb flexed one of his muscles. “I do like a challenge,” he admitted.

“Of course,” Howie said quietly, “you couldn’t straighten the leaning tower of Pisa in Italy. And it would be too hard for you to rebuild that crumbling coliseum in Rome.”

CHAMPION
OF THE

Howie noticed that Dr. Herb was frowning.

"There's a great big hole called the Grand Canyon," Howie said. "But filling that hole is just like fixing the coliseum and the tower. They're all jobs that even the strongest man in the world couldn't do. It would be too big of a challenge."

Dr. Herb scratched his chin as if he were thinking very hard. Then Dr. Herb leaned over Howie and went to work without saying a word.

13

Follow Your Dreams

The next morning Howie, Melody, and Liza rang Eddie's doorbell. They had to wait a long time before the door finally opened.

"Hurry up," Howie said. "You'll be late for your dentist appointment."

Eddie shook his head. "I'm not going," he said. "There's no way I'm letting that muscle man mess with my molars."

"You're his twelfth patient," Melody said.

"That's exactly why I'm not going," Eddie said.

"You have to go," Liza told him. "It wouldn't be polite to miss your appointment."

With his three friends pushing him the entire way, Eddie slowly made his way to

Dr. Herb's office. Silently, he pressed the button for the twelfth floor. By the time he reached office 1212, Eddie's face was as white as the teeth in his mouth.

As soon as the four kids entered the office, they knew something was wrong.

"The pictures are missing," Melody whispered. She was right. Not a single picture of a dog was left on the wall.

The receptionist called Eddie, but Eddie stopped before disappearing down the long hallway.

"You're not going to let me go by myself, are you?" Eddie asked.

But his friends didn't have a chance to answer because just then, a loud voice echoed into the waiting room. "Of course your friends can come with you," said the friendly voice.

"Dr. Zeus!" Liza screamed. "You're back."

Dr. Zeus stepped into the waiting room and grinned at the four friends. "I had to come back," he said. "I missed my patients too much!"

Eddie reached out and shook Dr. Zeus's hand so hard the white-haired man laughed. "I never thought I'd see the day when kids like you would be happy to see a dentist!"

"It's not just any dentist," Melody said. "We're happy to see *you*!"

"But what happened to Dr. Herb?" Howie asked. "He was supposed to check Eddie's teeth."

Dr. Zeus scratched his chin and shrugged. "I believe he found another job," he said, "in Italy."

"*Italy?*" Howie gasped. But Dr. Zeus didn't hear because he had already walked down the hall.

"My plan worked," Howie told Liza and Melody. "Dr. Herb has left Bailey City."

"But what if he comes back?" Liza asked.

"I don't think we'll see Dr. Herb for a long, long time," Howie said. "He'll be gone at least a couple of centuries."

"How do you know that?" Eddie asked.

Howie smiled. "Remember those cards Melody had?"

Liza and Eddie nodded. Melody pulled a stack of cards from her pocket.

"What do cards have to do with a dentist hightailing it out of his office?" Eddie asked.

"The cards told about Hercules' liking superhuman challenges," Howie said. "So I gave Hercules some challenges he couldn't resist."

"Thank goodness," Melody said. "Bailey City is safe now."

Eddie grabbed Melody's cards and held up the one of a creature with wild hair that looked like snakes. "We're okay," Eddie joked, "until Melody finds someone with crazy hair like this!"

Debbie Dadey and Marcia Thornton Jones have fun writing stories together. When they both worked at an elementary school in Lexington, Kentucky, Debbie was the school librarian and Marcia was a teacher. During their lunch break in the school cafeteria, they came up with the idea of the Bailey School kids.

Recently Debbie and her family moved to Aurora, Illinois. Marcia and her husband still live in Kentucky where she continues to teach. How do these authors still write together? They talk on the phone and use computers and fax machines!